THE GREAT RACE

STORY OF THE CHINESE ZODIAC

CHRISTOPHER CORR

Frances Lincoln
Children's Books

Long ago, in very ancient China, there were no years, or days, or hours.
The sun rose and fell without anyone knowing how much time
had passed, as there was no way of telling.

One day, the Jade Emperor realized that he did not know how old
he was. "We must have a way of measuring time!"
he thought.

So he gathered all the animals in the kingdom together and said,
"Tomorrow there will be a Great Race! The first twelve animals to cross
the river will each have a year named after them."

All the animals wanted to win this wonderful prize.

Among the animals were
the cat and the rat,
who were great friends.

"Let's win this race
together!" said the cat.
"Make sure you wake me
up," he added,
for he often slept all day.

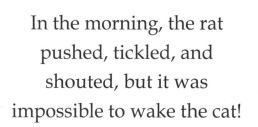

In the morning, the rat
pushed, tickled, and
shouted, but it was
impossible to wake the cat!

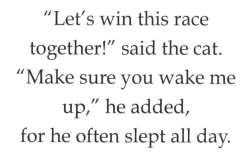

So he crept out of
the house and headed
for the river.

On his way, the rat met an ox. "Are you joining the race, Rat?" asked the ox. "Ride on my back, and I will carry you across."

"I will sing to you to say thanks," said the rat, and he climbed aboard.

The Great Race had begun! The big ox swam gracefully across the big river, serenaded by his new friend. But as soon as the rat saw land . . .

. . . he leapt from the ox
and fell at the feet of the Emperor.

"Congratulations, clever Rat!"
said the Emperor.

"The first year
will be named after you.
And the second year,
kind Ox, will belong
to you."

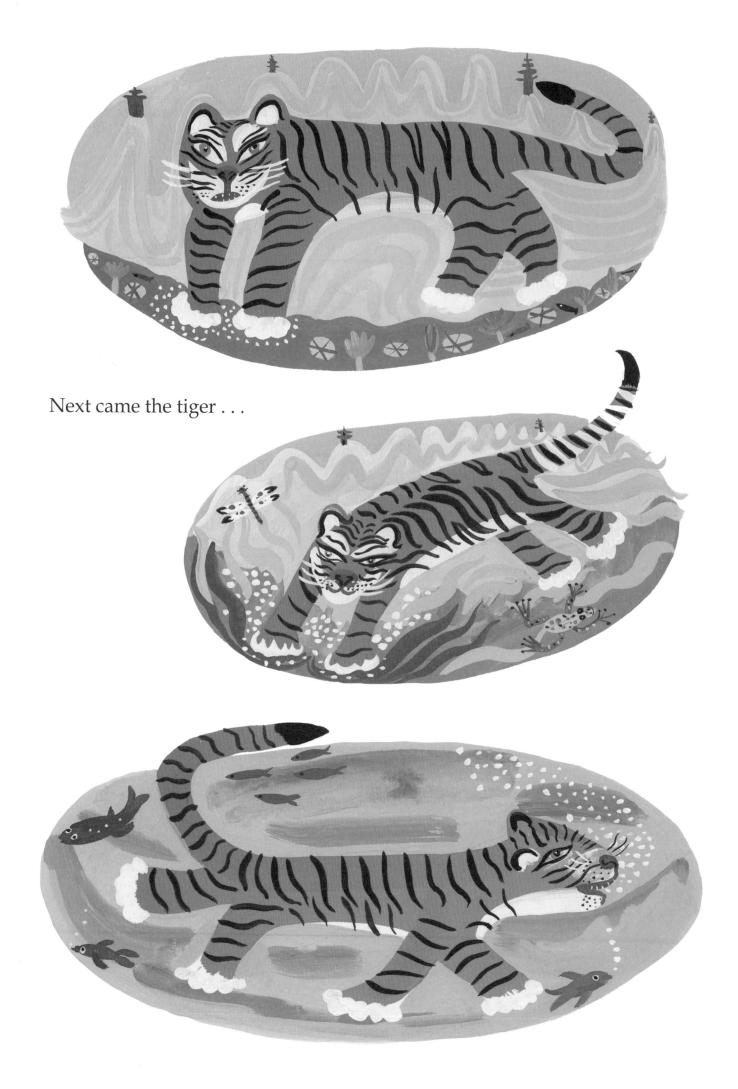

Next came the tiger . . .

whose beautiful striped
coat became heavy with
river water.

But the tiger struggled on
to reach the shore.

"Welcome, strong Tiger," said the Emperor. "The third year will be named after you."

The rabbit
really didn't like water.

He noticed some rocks
in the river, and decided to hop across
to keep his paws dry . . .

until a log floated by . . .

he jumped on, and a strong breeze
blew him ashore.

"The fourth year is named
after the lucky rabbit,"
said the Emperor.

A magnificent dragon was the fifth to cross the river.

"What kept you?" asked the Emperor.
"The land and the people were thirsty, so I had to make
rain for them," explained the dragon.

"And then I noticed a rabbit trying to cross the river,
so I blew a log in his direction and guided him to shore."

"Well, warm-hearted Dragon,"
said the Emperor, "the fifth year will belong to you."

Next, a galloping horse,
making waves and splashes,
appeared on the shore.

But just as he was shaking the water from his long mane,
a snake slithered from his leg!

The horse jumped back in fright,
and the crafty snake claimed sixth place.

"And you, fine Horse, have the seventh year!"
said the Emperor.

A goat, a monkey, and a rooster decided to work
together to win a place.

The rooster found a wooden raft.

The goat chewed weeds and grasses and cleared
a path for the raft to sail.

The monkey found a long branch which he used to
steer and push them to the other side.

The Emperor was delighted to see their fine teamwork.

"The eighth year will be Goat's,
the ninth year Monkey's,
and the tenth Rooster's," he said.

A dog arrived to claim eleventh place.

He was a strong swimmer, and could have arrived earlier,

but he was too busy chasing sticks and splashing in the water.
"The eleventh year will belong to the playful dog," called the Emperor.

As the moon was
rising in the evening
sky, the Emperor
heard a loud
squealing
and screeching.

It was a large pig
who finally emerged
from the river.

"I'm so sorry I'm late, Emperor,
but I found some delicious
apples by the riverbank and
then I found a pool of mud,
and then I fell asleep—"

"Be that as it may," said the Emperor,
"the twelfth and final year will
be the year of the pig."

"The Great Race is over!" said the Emperor.
"Let us celebrate."
But just then, there came a terrible howling from the reeds.

It was the cat, looking wet
and bedraggled and very, very cross.

He saw the rat sitting with the Emperor and shouted,
"You were supposed to wake me, you rat!
I will never forgive you!"

The cat was so angry that the rat fled for his life.

And through the first twelve years that passed, and the twelve years after
that, and all the many years leading up to this day . . .

rats have always fled from cats!